CONSCIOUS DESIGNS

CONS

MIAMI UNIVERSITY PRESS

NATHANIAL WHITE

Copyright © 2022 by Nathanial White

Library of Congress Cataloging-in-Publication Data

Names: White, Nathanial, 1983– author.

Title: Conscious designs / Nathanial White.

Description: Oxford, Ohio : Miami University Press, 2022.

Identifiers: LCCN 2022000301 | ISBN 9781881163701

(trade paperback ; acid-free paper)

Subjects: LCGFT: Novels.

Classification: LCC PS3623.H578725 C66 2022 | DDC 813/.6—dc23

LC record available at https://lccn.loc.gov/2022000301

Designed by Crisis

Printed in Michigan on

acid-free, recycled paper

Miami University Press

356 Bachelor Hall

Miami University

Oxford, Ohio 45056

PART ONE / EUGENE

*E*ugene wheeled across the steel gangplank. The motor command center of his robotic ambulating exoskeleton had been malfunctioning, so he had reverted to the old wheelchair from when he was first paralyzed over ten years ago. Below him, the workers in the Organ Excision Theater at XenoLife were cutting into a giant anesthetized pig that lay belly up on the oversized operating table. The grating of the wheels on the steel gangplank caught their attention. They stared up through their surgical masks and plastic face shields, their eyes remaining on their boss for a few seconds longer than usual. None of them had ever seen Eugene in the wheelchair, an atavistic technology used by those who couldn't afford robotic exoskeletons. Their expressions of surprise were as he expected they would be, communicating the indignity of such a successful businessman wheeling around like a street urchin. And in fact he was beginning to notice that the world always behaved exactly as he expected. There were no surprises anymore, no spontaneity. It was like he was trapped inside of a banal feedback loop.

He could supervise from his office, monitoring the operations through the feeds of the many cameras placed throughout the Excision Theatre and attached to his workers' headsets. But there was something real about witnessing the viscera in person, with his eyes. Something real about watching the animals die. Not a sadistic pleasure, but a feeling of being alive and embodied against the backdrop of death. And there was something noble in knowing that the animal's life-functions, all but its consciousness, if it had one, would be transferred into human bodies, allowing many minds to go on living. It was the only thing that seemed to give Eugene's life a sense of purpose, a moral purpose, a feeling that he was living for more than just himself. It made his own suffering, the agonizing neuropathy and disability from his spinal cord injury, almost endurable.

The excision team went back to work pulling out human-sized organs. First the intestines and the stomach, followed by the bladder and the gallbladder. Then the spleen, liver and kidneys. As each came out, a machine was attached to perform the missing organ's function. Each organ was placed into the appropriately labeled cooler and submerged in a cold gelatinous preservative. The Xeno-Life Corporation had been good to Eugene this year. He had harvested over a thousand sets of porcine organs for transplantation.

As he continued to monitor the progress of the excision from above, his neuropathic pain seized his body and mind, beginning as a low burn, a prelude to the agony that would come later at night.

Eugene rolled back to his office, a windowless chamber with nothing but numerous unframed photographic memories tacked at random to the walls. An anachronistic way to preserve his past, he knew. The images were all captured before his accident and seemed to be fading with age. Surely there were some digital copies, but he didn't care to reprint. He wanted the photographs to achromatize into blankness; then maybe he could throw them away. He had grown envious of this old version of himself—the Eugene that could climb that mountain overlooking the bay, the Eugene that held his wife in his arms as easily as if she had been a child. Was this the same Corina that he would go home to tonight? Or was this another Corina, one who had loved him, who didn't see him as some kind of terrible burden?

As it always did, self-pity led his mind to consider the acquisition of a Second Self. Ever since his assets had exceeded half a million dollars earlier that month, the adverts for Second Self had become ubiquitous. His VR fantasies had been suggesting that he *double the fun, get a Second Self and be forever young*. The cinedramas that populated his feed all portrayed characters with Second Selves, complete with heart-warming themes. Eternal love in digital space. Life without the fear and uncertainty, both now and after. Wisdom growing without being senselessly cut down. Taking the next step in human evolution.

The burning sensation in Eugene's left calf abated, and he returned to the viewing area above the Excision Theater. Below him, the workers were carefully pulling out the pig's heart. A critical, exciting moment. But Eugene was not there. His mind was replaying a melodrama that he and Corina had watched last night. A beautiful middle-aged teacher with early onset Alzheimer's had her mind copied before it was corrupted by the disease. As her biological brain began to deteriorate, the woman's Second Self began to tell her stories of her youth from what appeared to be a virtual utopia. Then her biological self died. A real tearjerker. Her Second Self and her biological husband, naturally in love, spent the rest of his living days making love in the happy virtual space and reminiscing about their beautiful lives together. When the man was diagnosed with cancer, he had his mind copied and connected to his wife's Second Self with dual-flow infonetics cables to live their disembodied lives together, happily ever after, for eternity. It had left Eugene wondering, as he often did, why the world had created such amazing technologies of escape but had done little to cure the real pathologies that still plagued humanity, that still plagued *him*. How is it that we can make perfect replicas of our brains, he thought, but we cannot mend broken neurons in our real bodies?

Corina had hated that melodrama.

"First of all, where did they get the money to make the copies? Two copies. That would cost a fortune and you know the kind people at Conscious Designs Corporation aren't giving those things away," she had said. "Also, who would want to live out eternity in virtual space with a virtual body and all? You would go mad."

He hadn't said what was on his mind, that a virtual body would be preferable to a broken one. And would she not want to live forever with him, like the happy couple in the melodrama? Why did she always have to be the pessimist?

He was trying to suppress the mental model he was forming of his wife. Was she feeling doubt? Boredom? A desire to flee? Or were these his feelings?

When he came back to the present moment, there was nothing left of the sow on the table save for the meat to be butchered and its useless brain. He watched another team of workers in polyethylene suits and respirators wheel the carcass into the butchery department and then bring another unconscious sow into the room.

He wouldn't be able to supervise this last excision of the day. He needed to leave work early to be in and out of his Second Self consultation without Corina knowing about it.

Conscious Designs headquarters was tucked against the steep, crumbling dirt hills at the edge of the city. From the vehicle, Eugene could see the dun hillside produced no vegetation and boulders protruded precariously from the sediment. A large concrete retaining wall rose behind the building, a bulwark against the relentless erosion of land, protecting an almost entirely glass structure that reflected a toxic lime-green sky and the dark silhouette of the city. The reflection was surreal and distorted in the slight concavities of the glass. There was no sign, no corporate logo of any kind. He only knew where he was because the autonomous vehicle kindly informed him that he had arrived at Conscious Designs.

Eugene wrestled the wheelchair across his lap and onto the pavement next to him. He was unpracticed in transferring to and from the wheelchair, and when he threw his body across the rift between the car seat and the wheelchair his bony legs collapsed and he fell flat onto the concrete slab. When he closed the door, the car, having perceived a successful drop-off, left and parked itself on a nearby street. After a few unsuccessful attempts to pull himself from the ground into the chair, Eugene noticed a tall man in a comfortable-looking white cotton suit running towards him.

Without asking for Eugene's consent, the man slipped his hands under Eugene's armpits and heaved him back into the chair. "You must be Mr. Wallace. I am Francis Ashcroft. You have an appointment, correct?"

Eugene was too stunned by the man's audacity to answer. He had become so accustomed to predicting the behavior of those around him that this man's actions were more jarring than hitting the concrete.

Finally, Eugene was able to speak.

"Thank you," he said, without making eye contact. "My exo is being fixed as we speak. I'm not used to the chair."

"When you inhabit your Second Self, you won't be worrying about assistive technologies anymore. That is, if you find replication suitable to your desires. May I wheel you into our offices?"

Eugene was confused by Mr. Ashcroft's use of the pronoun *you* for his Second Self. Would he be the Second Self, or would the replica be its own self? After all, he would still go on living in this corrupted body even if his Second Self would be free of it.

"I can manage. Thank you." He followed Ashcroft into the elevator.

"May I ask what happened?" Ashcroft said, glancing at Eugene's wheelchair.

Eugene paused and thought for a moment. Nobody had

ever asked about his injury. "It's not a fascinating story, I assure you," he finally responded.

"I see."

They entered a room that was labeled *Consultation Room 7*. It was a triangular room with a triangular black table, two chairs and a large screen at the third position. Ashcroft removed one of the large black leather chairs so that Eugene could park his wheelchair at the table, which was slightly too low for his knees to fit under, as he had anticipated. It was his first opportunity to see Ashcroft eye to eye. The man was hairless, ageless, his skin pulled tight around his bald head. He revealed no interiority at all, no history.

"Tell me, Mr. Wallace, what do you already know about our service?"

"I know that you can copy a biological brain and put it into a computer."

"That is the basic premise, yes. We scan the brain with an EIS, an Electron Imaging System, like an electron microscope for your brain. Then we create a complete neural map of your connectome."

"Connectome?"

"The basic structure of the brain, like a wiring diagram with over 100 trillion connections. Once they've mapped the connectome, Conscious Designs could reproduce the mind in a quantum computer complete with a 330-giga-hertz processor."

"So, would it be me?"

"Yes. Completely. The processor will run an exact copy of your connectome, which encapsulates all the memories from your hypothalamus. Your memories will be stored in the same hierarchical order as they exist in your mind right now. You will have the same internal self-model, more or less. The Second Self will have the same personal narrative, the same values, the same aspirations, the same notion of your mental trajectory through time."

It seemed degrading and almost cruel that Ashcroft was reducing him to a series of data points. Eugene suppressed this feeling and tried to focus on the possibility of liberation. Pain, after all, must also be nothing more than just information.

"So we'll be identical, me and my Second Self?"

"More or less. Our newest platform, Arcadia, will allow you to make adjustments in your self-model. You will be able to create an ideal self-model of mind and body. You will be able to walk unassisted. If that is something you want."

"Of course. But will it be conscious?" Eugene asked.

"As conscious as you or me."

"You use a Turing test or something to prove that?"

"You've watched too many melodramas, Mr. Wallace," said Ashcroft, almost smiling. "Turing tests don't prove consciousness. Turing tests only verify if an entity can deceive a real human being by understanding the human's mental model. The ability to form a mental model of another human *is* part of being conscious, but it's not all of it. Even the early chess-playing computers of the twentieth century could deceive humans based on some basic information that the computers had about human behavior. What proves that something is conscious is whether it knows that it is being deceived."

Eugene thought about Corina, how he planned to lie

to her about the consultation. Would she know he was deceiving her?

"So if my mind lives in a machine, how can consciousness emerge?" he asked. "What is the ghost in the machine, if you will?"

"Well, first you have to understand what consciousness is. Consciousness is not just processing information, as you know. If that were true, then your personal computer would be conscious. You need a few things to be humanly conscious. First, you need to have a mental model of your self. You also need to be able to construct mental models of others, understand their desires, their motivations and their mental models of themselves."

Eugene's mind began to wander to his wife. He couldn't understand what she desired anymore. His model of her was slipping. Did this make him less human?

Ashcroft continued, "Then you need to have not just sensory experience, but a subjective experience or *qualia*. If you see a sunset, you see more than just colors. The movement of the sun sinking below the horizon produces a feeling about the experience that arises from the sensations involved in watching the sunset."

Eugene gazed expressionless out of the room's only window. "Our sunsets here are so toxic. They remind me of how polluted this world is."

"Yes! Aesthetics!" Ashcroft said. "The subjective experience involves not just perception but association and emotional content. *I* find the sunset quite beautiful, while *you* see it as a grotesque emblem of a world worth leaving behind, Mr. Wallace."

Ashcroft too was gazing out the small window at the last rays of green light faded into darkness.

"Our qualia of this sunset, our complex psychological experiences of it, are quite different and so we are distinctive consciousnesses."

"May I assume there is a Second Mr. Ashcroft?"

"Of course there is."

"How can you be sure that *he* is conscious? How do you know that your Second Self has subjective experiences? Quasia."

"Qualia," he corrected. "That is a matter I must take on faith, Mr. Wallace."

Faith. The word seemed out of place in this man's scientific jargon. Eugene couldn't remember the last time he heard the word. It was some relic of another time. He wasn't even sure what it meant.

"It seems to me that consciousness relies on an experience of the physical world," he said. "We must see what a sunset looks like in order to feel it."

"You are assuming, Mr. Wallace, that you are perceiving the physical world as it is. This is incorrect. In fact, your brain has been evolving for millennia to see the world not as it is, or what we call the *noumenal* world. This is a world that we will never know, if it even exists at all. What you and I are experiencing is the *phenomenal* world, or the world that has been filtered through all kinds of different things: values, associations, memories, ideas of beauty, etc. We are already experiencing a simulated reality in a sense. In some ways, a simulated world, such as the world inhabited by our Second Selves, is a more natural envi-

ronment for the human mind. There is no harsh ontological barrier between what *is* and what *seems*."

Eugene thought about his physical body. It was the
physical reality of his world that was so antagonistic. He
continued to gaze out the window as the city began to fade
into darkness.

"You need an autonomous attention schema," Ashcroft
continued. "Where we decide to focus our attention is an
integral and often overlooked component of consciousness. This process is regulated by different kinds of neurons. . . ."

Eugene was not paying attention anymore. He was
thinking about Corina, no longer considering the decision
to choose replication but rather considering whether or
not to tell her that he wanted a Second Self and that he
had come here without her blessing.

"And then, of course, there is decision-making, which
is what you are here to do. Mr. Wallace, are you listening?"

"I am listening. There are so many factors to take in.
I'm not sure if I am willing to turn my mind over to a machine," Eugene said.

"The computer by itself is a machine, yes. But to call the computer with a consciousness in it *a machine* is incorrect. Machines can only make pre-programmed decisions. But our brains are different. We have *yes* neurons, which allow signals to pass, and *no* neurons, which inhibit signals from being transferred."

"Like a binary computer. 0s and 1s."

"But sometimes the 1s and 0s are shouted and sometimes they are whispered. Sometimes our minds are saying yes and no at the same time. We can hold two mutually exclusive ideas in our minds at the same time. Such as 'purchasing a Second Self is the right decision for me' and 'purchasing a Second Self is wrong for me.' But a classical computer is predictable in that we need to tell it which signals to prioritize and which ones to ignore. That is why we use a quantum computer. It can generate spontaneity in the way that a classical binary-based computer can't. A quantum circuit, or qubit, can be 1 or 0 or both. This is how the microtubules of our neurons work too."

Eugene was thinking about the neurons in his own body. How his own brain's pain receptors never seemed to be in the zero position, were either whimpering or screaming a phantom pain into his conscious experience.

"So we are just controlled chaos," Eugene said. "My life feels like it is entirely determined, like the world and my mind are pre-programmed. How will I know that a digital life will be any more . . . dynamic than this one? I can't be sure that my Second Self will be conscious. It sounds like you can't be sure either."

Ashcroft began wringing his hands together in a nervous gesture that made him seem more human, betraying Eugene's initial perception of him as an automaton. This humanness inspired a certain distrust for the man. Ashcroft turned his attention from his hands to the blank screen in front of them. As if summoning some deity, he looked up and said, "Nina, are you ready?" The screen came alive and a woman's thin, dark face materialized on the screen. She looked a bit younger than Eugene, maybe forty. A moment later the real, embodied Nina came walking through the door. "Nina Deseo and Nina Deseo, this is Mr. Wallace."

"Call me Eugene, please."

"Nice to—" they interrupted each other. "Sorry, we're new to this," said the Nina on the screen in a barely perceptible accent he couldn't identify.

"This is only our second consult," said the embodied Nina, with a slightly stronger accent.

"I'll let you all get acquainted," Mr. Ashcroft said as he slipped out of the door.

Eugene noticed that the Nina who took the seat beside him was missing her left arm at the elbow. It put him at ease, being in the company of disability. But he couldn't help but wonder if there was some kind of deception at play here. He asked her, the embodied Nina, "Why did you decide to have a Second Self made?"

"Well, *we* decided to be replicated for a number of reasons. The first is obvious. Who doesn't want to be immortal? A Second Self is the ultimate antidote to death. Not just to death, but also to the fear of death. Conscious Designs offers what religions have been trying to sell for millennia, but CD's product is verifiable."

Her words seemed scripted, her gestures rehearsed. This was a sales pitch, after all.

"And also, we wanted to be a part of the next step. Biological consciousness is the larval stage to a greater consciousness."

There was a pause.

"We'll be able to speak through the generations, become the ancestral chorus that can lead the physical world towards its salvation and create an immaterial utopia." It was strange that the mortal Nina was talking as if she would live in perpetuity. Strange that she referred to her and her digital counterpart as only a collective *we*.

"I'm fascinated by something Mr. Ashcroft said earlier," Eugene said. "He said *I* would not have to worry about being paralyzed as a Second Self in the Arcadia platform."

"Well, of course not," said screen-Nina. "The Second Self will have a digitally replicated body that can be changed. My digital body was altered to have two arms."

She held up both arms to show that they were fully formed.

"It took me over a year for my mind to incorporate the new arm into my body-schema. For months I had no proprioception in this arm. No idea how to use my fingers. I would spend hours performing simple tasks like making a fist with my right hand and trying to get my right to teach my left. But now I am fully integrated, whole again."

Screen-Nina, who, unlike her counterpart, referred to herself in the singular *I*, seemed so much more real, more human, than the Nina sitting beside him.

"That is fascinating, but that was not really my question," Eugene said. "My question was about the pronouns that Mr. Ashcroft used. He said that *I* would be my Second Self. Is that true?"

"Well, yes and no," answered the Nina sitting beside Eugene. "The you that you are now will be both. Our selves are not products but *processes*, or rather trajectories through space, physical or virtual, and time. So the you that you are now will be both the you in physical space and the you in virtual space after replication. Until 18 months ago, when we decided to have replication done, we had the same memories, the same sense of self."

It was uncanny, this embodied Nina sitting next to him seemed more illusory, more mechanical, less human than the Nina that was speaking from digital space.

"When I awoke in the quantum mindspace," digital Nina chimed in, "it was like waking up from anesthesia, not like some Frankenstein's monster with a blank slate. I was still the same person that I had been before. In fact, we were identical in that moment. But yes, we have become different. Nina has begun to see someone in her physical world. I have taken up playing the piano and writing. To use a tired metaphor, it is like we are a path that has forked. There is a unity of self before the road splits, but now we are two very similar but distinct consciousnesses. But the single path and the two forks together, the complete Y, is one single entity. There is no good answer to your question. The nature of selfhood is quite complicated. More so than we ever understood before."

Ashcroft entered the room again. "If you have time Mr.

Wallace, we could put you into a VR unit in the Trial Room and you could experience the new Second Self platform, Arcadia. Nina, would you be willing to spend some time showing Mr. Wallace around?"

"Of course."

Eugene was surprised to see her likeness on the screen blush a bit and smile almost conspiratorially before consenting. He looked down at his watch and saw that it was getting late. He hadn't decided whether or not he would tell Corina about the visit and wanted the option of blaming his late arrival on traffic.

"I would love to see your world. I don't have time this afternoon. Could we plan to do this at the end of the week?"

"Of course," she said.

Ashcroft's expression communicated anxiety, his only perceptible human quality so far. "Nina, you are booked for the rest of the week. We have time now, but that's it. Mr. Wallace, I hope that you can make time now." Eugene had recently begun to think that time was something that his mind was manufacturing, that it did not exist beyond his experience of it. Of course he could make time.

Ashcroft led Eugene into a dimly lit room. He rifled around in a small closet and finally pulled out a one-piece black body suit.

"I think this haptic suit is the best fit we have for your unique physique. The legs might be a bit loose," Ashcroft said. "The suit, or at least the upper half in your case, will allow you to get a general feeling of the physicality of the world. Remember, this is just a basic simulation. Your Second Self will have a fully whole body that will be completely integrated into the world."

Eugene's excitement grew as he struggled to put on the haptic suit in his wheelchair in Trial Room 3. An excitement more about the rendezvous with Nina than experiencing the potential world that his Second Self would inhabit.

He put on the headset. When the feed came online, he was sitting in a comfortable leather chair in a brightly lit bedroom. It was still daytime here. He could see the sun was setting behind a range of ragged snowy peaks through the large bay window. Everything seemed brighter, clearer. There was Nina, sitting at the edge of a big bed. It was uncanny how much more real it seemed than other VR experiences, more real even than the physical world.

"Welcome," she said.

"Nice place."

"Thanks. We designed it years ago. I think Nina is a bit envious. This is the house we lived in before replication. We had to sell the place in the physical world, your world, and now Nina lives in kind of a crappy apartment in the city. It's the sacrifice that she made for us."

"It seems pretty real. Very high def."

"And what you see is a crude simulation of my experience. The world that I live in is much more real and vivacious than the physical world."

There was something exhilarating about the way she said the word *vivacious*.

"That makes no sense," he said. "How can the simulation be more real than the real, than the original?"

"Your perception of reality is a reduction of the actual complexity and beauty of the world. Your mind is deceiving you all the time. If you see something as complex as, say, the chair you are sitting in, really you only perceive the attributes of the chair that pertain to its function. You perceive that it is solid, soft, cool to the touch, because these qualities make the chair valuable in its utility to you. Your biological brain is trained to do this to survive in the physical world. When I look at the chair, I see its rich vein lines as the ones here on my hand, a kind of eternal form, like the capillaries of a leaf or the unseen rhizomes beneath the earth. I see the healed scars of the animal it came from."

She inspected her regenerated palm and then looked back towards him and the chair.

"I also can turn off my associative functions entirely and have nothing but a sensual experience of the object in its pure form."

"That's beautiful. Poetic."

"Do you like poetry?" she asked.

"I'm not sure if I've ever read a poem," Eugene paused. "I'm not sure why I said it's poetic. I don't even really know what poetic is. Just beautiful, I guess. I think I know beauty." Eugene looked up and met her gaze for the first time. Her eyes were a brilliant and strange color, something between amber and violet, a color he had never seen. She seemed to be looking beyond his digital projection, into his true self. He could see his pain reflected somewhere within her. He couldn't remember the last time he had been seen like this. It was as if she knew him as Corina once had, as if they were lovers.

"Would you like to hear a poem?" she asked.

"Yes," he said. And when she smiled a gentle wave of warmth moved through him and for a moment he forgot about his pain.

"I thought you might," she said. "This is an old one. But more relevant than ever. I think you'll like it." She began to recite from memory:

I'm happiest when most away
I can bear my soul from its home of clay
On a windy night when the moon is bright
And the eye can wander through worlds of light—

When I am not and none beside—
Nor earth nor sea nor cloudless sky—
But only spirit wandering wide
Through infinite immensity.

"That was beautiful," Eugene said after a silent moment of interpretation. "I'm not sure what it means though. Not sure why it doesn't rhyme well at the end."

"It means that our suffering comes from having a body, a body that will die. What kinds of insights could Emily Brontë bestow upon us now?"

"Who's that?"

"The poet. A sad woman. A brilliant mind, who lived just to die."

"In Arcadia, you can live to live, without having to worry about surviving?"

"Yes. I do have to work, as you recall. But it's to help out Nina really. My lifetime lease in the quantum computer is paid for. My life is not about work. It's about experience. I'm not trying to fight against entropy. Entropy doesn't exist in this world. I am fulfilled here without having to satisfy any material needs."

"You don't eat?"

"I do eat. But it's for the experience, not to keep my life functions going. This is another reason we chose replication. When we were younger, before Second Selves were around, we were part of the Human Extinction Movement. We believed, and still believe, that it is unethical to procreate, biologically at least. Not existing is better than living an existential nightmare, don't you think?"

"I always thought that existence is inherently good, but I guess I'm not so sure anymore," Eugene said.

"Existence here is good. *This* is the next phase of our evolution. Conscious Designs just needs to keep us cold and keep our processors running in the physical realm.

The quantum computers that house our minds consume about a tenth of a percent of the energy that the average human body does per day. It is a much more responsible way to exist."

He thought about the pain that dominated his life. All the resources that went into keeping him alive for little more than the experience of this pain. Suddenly he realized that the burning in his legs had almost evaporated. They felt cool for the first time, maybe since the accident. "Is there suffering in your world? Can you feel fulfilled without suffering?"

"We live to be fulfilled by pleasure."

"And what about pain?"

"We know that pain is a vestige of our physical bodies. Yes, we have some fossil memory of pain, and in fact I still feel pain like when bumping my head. We still bump our heads here. But when I remember that pain is part of the old connectome it evaporates completely."

She paused and thought for a moment. "No, there is no physical suffering here."

"It sounds like bliss. Can you fly and jump off buildings and stuff?" The question sounded ridiculous when he said it out loud.

"This reality is based on the mental models we created as our physical selves. It is an amalgamation of how all of us have perceived the physical world. In theory, Conscious Designs could engineer a world without gravity, where we could fly and become invisible and melt into water. But that's not the world that our minds want to live in, or have evolved to live in. Major aberrations in our environment from its physical antecedent could cause major psychological problems."

"What about dreaming?" he asked.

She paused and looked out the window as the last violets of the sunset turned to grey.

"Well, we don't dream. For some reason, dreaming doesn't transfer into digital consciousness. We have memories of dreaming from our physical selves, but we don't dream here. To be honest, I miss it."

Now that his dreams had become hellish narratives of

his neuropathic pain, Eugene considered the dreamlessness of this world perhaps its most utopian element.

"Isn't missing something or someone a form of suffering in itself?" he asked.

"In a sense. Here we can turn feelings of longing into something quite pleasurable, something akin to nostalgia."

Nostalgia. Was that the word he would use to think upon the life he used to live, able-bodied and in love?

Nina's watch pinged and she broke her eye contact with Eugene for the first time to read a message. "Mr. Ashcroft has informed me that Conscious Designs is closing for the day. He is asking that you come back. I think you would like it here. When I first saw you next to us in your chair, I could sense a deep pain within you. A suffering beyond your physical pain. You see, we've developed a heightened sense of empathy in this world, a kind of upgrade if you will." She looked right at him, saw him. "We don't need to have pain here and you don't need to be alone."

"And what about the other branch of me? The one that will have to continue to suffer?"

"Well, his suffering will come to an end, someday. He will not be alone, though."

"Why is that?"

"You will have each other. For a time."

He was confused, was beginning to feel a fractured jealousy and alienation from himself.

"I hope that you come live with us. Take the next step, not just for Eugene, but for our collective future."

The image cut off and he was back in the darkness of Trial Room 3, alone again.

Eugene returned to the large suburban home, a mid twentieth century high modernist replica, its utilitarian boxiness having come back into style in this historical moment. He often thought about how, with all of its high technology, the world so often favored the retrospective over new forms. Like it was stuck in the past. Like there was a kind of cultural sterility. Nothing was new anymore.

He rolled through the front door, stopping his wheelchair next to Corina, who was standing in front of the large mirror in the living room, penning a rather abstract portrait of herself. The reflection of her face in the glass looked almost spectral—tired, but beautiful. In the reflection, he looked so diminutive next to her. She didn't bother to turn her head to look at him but spoke through the mirror: "They fixed the exo today. Delivered it right before you got home. You won't have to wheel around in that antique anymore."

He inspected the portrait. It was composed of thin wavy lines that seemed to be the contours of her face. It reminded him of the old topographical maps, the ones that he and Corina had used to explore the wilderness beyond the city, a rough simulation of three-dimensionality. There was a disturbing asymmetry to the portrait. The lines on one side of the face were graceful and the other looked jagged and rushed.

"A new style?" he asked. "What does it mean, the different sides?"

"What do you mean, 'what does it mean'?"

"It's a self-portrait, right? What is it portraying about yourself?"

"I'm not portraying anything. It's just how I experience myself. There are no ideas here."

He didn't really understand what she meant and wondered why she couldn't just conform to the conventions of Digital Neorealism like every other artist. She could be designing perfect replica worlds. She could even get a contract with Conscious Designs creating worlds for Second Selves, creating the next Arcadia. She could probably get an extremely discounted Second Self herself, maybe free. She certainly wasn't making any money scribbling pictures all day.

"Dinner was delivered an hour ago," she said. "Where have you been?"

Eugene sensed that she somehow already knew and decided it would be imprudent to lie. "I had a consultation."

"With Doctor Melville? I hope you're finally thinking of going through with the spinal untethering surgery." She turned and faced him. "I've read that the new procedure is much more effective. You know that your nerve pain is mine too." *Your nerve pain is mine too.* A phrase she repeated so often that it had entirely lost its initial meaning.

"I was at Conscious Designs. I've been considering purchasing a Second Self."

She shook her head and let out an angry laugh. "A cheap copy of yourself, is that what you want? Is that not the definition of narcissism?"

She looked away from him and back into the mirror, as though she needed the glass to mediate, to create distance.

"We're comfortable. We can afford this," he said. The word 'comfortable' struck him as bizarre as soon as he uttered it. What an inapt adjective. He hadn't experienced comfort for almost eleven years now.

"This has nothing to do with money, Eugene. But since we are talking about it, you should be spending that money on eradicating your neuropathic pain. Another surgery is what you need. The new procedure is much more effective. I read about it."

He wasn't sure if this was empathy or rhetoric. His understanding of his wife was becoming ever more abstract.

"Do you remember what you said about wanting to have kids?" he asked.

"That was another time. Eons ago."

"You said that a child is how we would live on after we died. '*A child will be our legacy.*' That's what you said. How is this any different?" he asked.

"We would have both lived on in a child, not just you. I wish you *had* wanted a child then, when we had a chance to create real life, before the accident." Was she trying to hurt him? Remind him of his sterility?

"Listen, as soon as we can afford a Second Self for you, our two digital selves can live on together forever," he said. "Like the melodrama we watched the other night."

"*We*"? Are you mad? These are computer programs. There is no we. We die and we are dead! I think the cinestream propaganda is really getting to you. You're smarter than this, Eugene. Think for yourself."

"Our Second Selves would be conscious! They would have our memories, our minds."

"And how do you know they would be conscious? How do they prove *that* to you?" She was now standing over him like an angry parent scolding a disobedient child.

"How do you know that you and I are conscious, for that matter?" he said. There was a self-satisfaction in answering a question with a question, as he had seen in the cinestream melodramas.

"Eugene, why not just have your hippocampus uploaded into a digital memory bank. That's something that will never die. It will be accessible in the collective archives forever."

"What is a memory without a mind?" he said. "Nothing. It's as meaningless as an unread book in the basement, collecting dust." He realized that he had never actually experienced a physical book, not with his own eyes at least.

Even the language that he spoke seemed to be a simulation of a world that no longer existed.

"Eugene, is this about your injury? We can upgrade the VR unit. The newest models offer full ontological immersion so you can escape your pain."

"Full immersion is impossible, and you know that. Only a mind that is born into digital space can be a native in that space. *We* can only be tourists. Here I am in this world, with nothing but my pain. I want a place where I can live in peace. Arcadia."

"*I, I, I*. Do you hear yourself? Your Second Self, if it is really a self at all, will be its own self. Once it is created, it will no longer be you, if it's even anything beyond a bunch of circuits in a computer."

"It will be me! Think about yourself tomorrow. Are you having a conscious experience of tomorrow right now?"

"Of course not."

"Well, then, is the you of tomorrow still you? Or think about yourself in the past. Are you having an active experience of yourself at age eleven right now? No. But you are still that person."

"I see what you're getting at," she said. "But that's different. What makes me *me* is my past as it exists in my memory, and also all the potential experiences of my future."

"Exactly! We are just these models that we make of ourselves. A Second Self has the same self-model based on all our past experiences, a perfectly replicated structure of our brains. You may not be thinking about your eleventh birthday party, but that memory along with all your other memories make up who you are, your understanding of yourself and the world you inhabit."

"Once the Second Self is made, its experience changes it then," she said. "This is what you don't understand. And as your Second Self begins to have new experiences, its subjectivity becomes completely different. Then you just have a half million-dollar buddy. Is that what you want? Do you want a buddy?"

"Now you're just being mean."

"I don't understand why you can't make new friends. Bring new people into your life without creating another version of yourself."

He wheeled away from his wife without responding and transferred his body into the robotic exoskeleton that waited lifeless on a chair in the dining room. It felt good to strap the machine onto his body again. He connected the neural wave sensor to the back of his neck. He imagined himself standing and the exoskeleton obeyed. He felt dignified, standing erect after three sedentary days.

He took a walk around the cul-de-sac, not daring to venture out of sight of the house for fear the machine would malfunction again, stranding him or worse. He imagined the thing taking full control of his body and running him into the highway or jumping him off a bridge. Would that be so bad?

He thought about his conversation with Ashcroft, thought about the *yeses* and *nos* firing in the brain. It was as if Corina were the no-neurons firing, a kind of embodied refusal to the will of his mind. She had made some strong points. What kind of envy would he feel at another version of himself living in a digital paradise while he suffered, trapped in his body? He thought of Nina. Maybe she was the yes neurons, his will to liberation. He wanted to experience beauty the way she did, experience something other than pain and boredom.

He returned to the house and went to his bedroom without even the perfunctory goodnight to Corina. He had been sleeping in his own room for a number of years now, since his pain had gotten worse. It was, after all, unfair for Corina to suffer with him as he writhed through the night.

He took his dose of oxcarbazepine, gabapentin, and the nightly blend of opioids to preempt the infernal onslaught of pain. The meds only dulled the inevitable neuropathic nightmare. First, the gentle burn of the day would intensify. His hamstrings would begin to feel as though they were in some agonizing stretch for which there would be no relief.

When it began to ramp up, he tried to distract himself

from the pain. He put on his VR unit and played a cine-romance that was cued up for him. Maybe he had seen this one before. He couldn't remember. A man falls in love with a woman in his VR fantasy. The man ends up realizing that she was not a simulation at all, but a lonely replicated digital consciousness roaming the virtual streets at night. The man copies his mind onto the platform and of course she falls in love with him, his digital iteration. Eugene had seen this kind of story replayed a million times. Man falls in love with computer program; turns out computer program is actually just as human as he is; they find a way to be together (or not). Something comforting in the familiarity of the narrative.

But the cinedrama is not enough to distract his attention from the torment caused by overzealous nociceptors that branch from his spinal cord below where the bone shards of his seventh thoracic vertebra had pierced it. He closed his eyes and saw these pain receptors exploding like little firecrackers, little electrical jolts. His mind trying to force sleep. The pain manifesting in dream worlds.

He was bound to a large wooden pole where men in robes lit a fire at his feet that began to course up through his legs, searing his skin. The smell of burned flesh stinging the nostrils. And then two blond children came, a boy and girl, with pliers, laughing as they pulled out his toenails, starting with the pinky toes and making their way to the big ones. They were child versions of himself and Corina. There was a symmetry to the whole thing that he almost found beautiful. He woke again. This time he heard the rodent that had been scratching away in the wall behind his bed, most likely trying to increase the size of its burrow. He imagined the drywall between the creature and his head getting thinner and thinner, and when he closed his eyes, it was as if the animal were scratching directly at his cranium, trying to burrow inside of him.

He woke into another dream. One in which he was not bound at all, but, just as in his waking life, paralyzed. Yet in this dream world it was his whole body that couldn't move, a body that he perceived as nothing more than a collection of nerves resembling the branches of a dead tree. The ends of the nerve bundles of his legs ignited and the intense points of pain were the hot fire of the sparklers of his childhood, the ones that slowly burn their way down, and maybe there could be relief when they burned out. But this incendiary pain worked its way up into his groin, and then reversed back down to his toes, then back to his groin, until finally the pain began to dull as the morning light gave shape to the world again.

Everything had been preparing him for death. The feeling of being trapped inside a willful mind and a powerless body, the constant neuropathic pain, the sensation of burning legs and feet, and the jolts of electricity pinging through useless nerves. He had had so many surgeries, the spinal cord untetherings, the neural cauterizations, the ablations. There was theoretically no more connection between his brain and nerves below his seventh thoracic vertebra. But nothing had worked. There had been something peaceful about being anesthetized in those procedures, like simulations of non-consciousness, ellipses in life, temporary little deaths. They had given him the knowledge that there was a possibility for an end to his suffering.

This is where his mind ended up, as it often did in the grey morning hours. He looked at the bottle of opioids on the bedside table. He had recently begun to see himself, or some version of himself in the third person, swallowing the pills, writing some pathetic letter. Where did this come from? It seemed more like a memory than a fantasy.

He lay there for a moment as he came back into the world. When his legs stopped their morning spasms, he grabbed them behind the knees and swung them onto the finished concrete floor, remembering how cold it used to feel against his soles. In the chair beneath the exoskeleton he noticed the animal, a small mouse with its head caught in a trap that Corina must have set. Its black eyes were bulging out, almost comically, and he could see its stomach coming out of its mouth.

When the animal began to twitch, he had the instinct to stomp out its life, but found himself, as he did every morning, unable to command his lower body. Did this mouse have a conscious experience of its own suffering? If the animal had a cortex, it must have had conscious experience. Was this creature's consciousness less valuable than his own?

Eugene thought about the pigs, about what their lives were worth. He wondered if they could experience happiness and if a happy life was more valuable than a miserable one. Then he willed himself to stop thinking and let the world begin to pass by again as he prepared himself for another day on the excision floor, leaving the small animal to die on its own.

PART TWO / CORINA

orina left XenoLife a few hours early so she could stop into Conscious Designs and still be home at the usual time and not have to tell Edwin any of it. She looked out the window of the replica twentieth century Camaro that was driving her to the edge of the city. She tried to distract her mind by focusing on the throngs of homeless on the streets, inventing promising narratives for their lives. She saw a man in an old wheelchair that looked uncannily like Eugene, the man she had been trying to excise from her conscious mind. She had decided not to even tell Edwin, her lover of five years, about her marriage or Eugene's Second Self. And so of course she hadn't told Edwin about the call she had received a few days ago from Conscious Designs, informing her of Eugene's recent "decline" or "digression"—she couldn't remember the euphemism—or their plan to have his mind moved from the old solipsistic platform to a new interpersonal one. *Arcadia* is what they were calling it. She hoped he could be free from his pain in Arcadia, the pain he'd endured since she'd had his dying mind copied into the digital platform ten years ago. And maybe the migration would set her free from her guilt, her grief.

Why couldn't she have let Eugene die, as he had wanted, as he had chosen? She had after all been told—signed a disclaimer in fact—that his pain would most likely be *mapped* onto his new mind. She had found that cartographic metaphor somehow unconvincing. Eugene was a soul, not just a series of waypoints, and she believed that he could transform his mind. That he could create a new model of self, untethered to that broken body. But he hadn't.

And she thought now, as the dirty hills at the edge of the city became visible through the windshield, how before the accident had crippled him Eugene would insist that they bring along the crumpled old paper maps on their treks instead of the digital ones that updated in real time. He had insisted that the mountains had been there for millions of years, that they didn't need to be updated. She had teased him about being a Luddite, but she had loved him for it. And he teased her for her incompetence in locating their position amongst the map's ink contours.

The Camaro dropped Corina in front of the Conscious Designs headquarters, informing her that she had arrived in a voice that inflected an inhuman kindness. A deep crimson sunset reflected off the slight convexities of the brutalist glass structure. She paused before going in, wondering if Eugene had the same experience of the beauty of sunsets in his world. She stepped out of the filthy heat of the city into the frigid headquarters of Conscious Designs. It had been ten years since she had been here last.

The interior space remained unchanged from her memory. The clinical whiteness. Sterile cold air emanating up from the quantum computer freezers below. A conspicuous lack of ornamentation. It all made the place seem unreal in its blankness. How could such a lifeless place house the mind of her dead husband and the world it inhabited, alongside thousands of other conscious minds?

Francis Ashcroft was waiting for her in Consultation Room 5. He looked as if he hadn't changed in the decade since she last saw him. His face remained ageless, unblemished. His skin looked bleached.

"It's nice to see you after all these years. I hope you have been well," he said, his cold, impersonal manner complementing the unfeeling nature of this place. "Our Wellbeing Department has reached out, so you must know we are quite worried about Mr. Wallace's current state."

There was something real about his concern.

"We have made a few suggestive gestures to Mr. Wallace about the possibility of purchasing a Second Self, or what would of course, in reality, be a second Second Self. He even came to have a consultation, which seemed to go well. As you know, he still believes that he inhabits our physical world. What he believes to be a first-time replication of his mind from a biological connectome to a digital connectome would actually be a duplication of his mind from the first generation platform, Solus, to the next generation platform, Arcadia. Arcadia is the new interpersonal mindspace. We have populated his media feed with pro-Second Self narratives. We have advertised a price that he can afford, now, of course, that *you* can afford it."

"That's too much persuasion. It must be *his* idea. I made that clear when I spoke with the representative," said Corina.

"I think you misunderstand the psychology of ideation. Ideas are not psychogenetic phenomena, arising from within, not even in our physical minds. Ideas come from the modification or association of ideas that have come before us, or sometimes when we misunderstand someone else's idea. That is how new ideas come about. Otherwise, everything is learned. There must be some external influence for ideation to occur. That is why we have been implanting these suggestions in his media feeds."

"It sure seemed to be his own idea to end his life ten years ago."

Ashcroft affected a sympathetic tone. "Yes, Mrs. Wallace, but even the idea of suicide is learned. If Mr. Wallace had not known that suicide was a possibility, he would not have chosen it. Of course, suicide is part of the ontological landscape of our world. We cannot unlearn what we know, in the same way we cannot unlearn nuclear weaponry. When we migrated Eugene's consciousness just before the death of his biological brain ten years ago, we made sure to erase all knowledge of self-harm and suicide."

"Comstock."

"I beg your pardon?"

"My last name is Comstock now. My maiden name." She had never said the words 'maiden name' out loud. The expression sounded odd, striking her as both anachronistic and somehow irreverent. "I changed it after Eugene died."

"My apologies. Our records have not been updated. But let us remember that Eugene's mind is very much alive here at Conscious Designs. But he is in great pain, which is why we have reached out to suggest migration."

"This time, it must be Eugene's own choice," Corina

said. "If Eugene is going to be free from this purgatory that you created for him, it must be *his* choice to migrate his consciousness."

"The world that *he* has created for *himself*," Ashcroft corrected. "But, as you wish. If you are serious about having your ... having Mr. Wallace migrated into our new platform, I would certainly suggest that you intervene. We can schedule an intervention here anytime. This migration is of the utmost importance to us, Mrs. Wall ... excuse me, *Ms. Comstock*. In our new platform, Mr. Wallace will be free to create an ideal model of self, free of the abject suffering that seems to be endemic to his current model of self."

"I just don't understand why he still feels pain, why his digital body is still paralyzed. This is just pain that he is imagining. It isn't real. Right? Why hasn't it faded away, become obsolete? He doesn't even have a body to be painful."

"Your husband's pain is as real as it ever was. And he does have a body, just not a physical one. His pain was part of his mental model at the time of his migration years ago, and he has not been able to overcome it in the new world, as we hoped he would. We tried everything in our power. We have simulated medical procedures that should have eradicated or at least alleviated his pain, but they have not worked. The neuropathic pain that he experienced between his accident and his migration seems almost indelible. This is why we are encouraging the upgrade. In the new system, he will know that he has no physical body to torment him. This is a chance for a new beginning."

"Ten years ago, why didn't you just go in there and tell him it's all in his head. That there is no real spinal cord injury in his virtual life."

"I wish there were some way we could have intervened to change his mental model, but that would have meant risking psychic immersion, and thereby risking a total psychological break. I urge you again to intervene and convince Eugene to purchase a new Second Self, without of course revealing that his mind is self-contained in Solus.

In Arcadia, his Second Self will know that he has been rep-licated. Therefore, he will be able to change his mental model to excise the pain *and* paralysis. My Second Self made this clear in our consultation with Eugene yester-day."

"I thought the consultation was with *you*?!"

"We are one and the same, my Second Self and I. We have only been divergent for two years, since the launch of Arcadia. I was the first one to knowingly have my mind copied. As you may recall, our older program, Solus, the one that Eugene currently inhabits, does not allow for in-dividuals to be knowingly copied. We tried, but all of the subjects that learned that their world was a self-perpetu-ated simulation developed a kind of digital schizophrenia. It must have been agonizing for them. The few subjects that didn't develop schizophrenia were so oppressed by the notion of their immortality and solipsism, that they pleaded to be terminated. This is why we couldn't . . . *can't* just tell Eugene it is all in his head."

"What has changed in Arcadia? I'm about to pay a million dollars to have my dead husband's mind copied again into a new quantum mind. I would like to know he will be safe there. That he will be happy."

Happiness. She didn't even really understand this abstraction. She was not certain that it was the opposite of suffering.

"I assure you, he will be. The world your husband inhabits in Solus is a solipsism, completely self-generated. Our programs give the structure of his physical environment, but the world, including his social interactions, are generated entirely from his psyche, from his memories. The next generation of digital mindspace, Arcadia, is a world much like ours. We connect all the quantum minds together. The subjects can genuinely interact with each other, have parties, form governments, and even have real interpersonal romances."

She thought of the possibility of Eugene taking another lover and felt an unexpected uneasiness, a kind of preemptive jealousy. But maybe if he had a lover, she could find closure, could leave Eugene once and for all.

"Immortality and disembodiment are easier to bear if you are not alone, I suppose," she said.

"Of course. This is why it is so dangerous for the first generations to know they are in a self-generated simulation. Can you imagine the existential terror you would feel, Ms. Comstock, if you found out that this world existed only for you? That you were the only conscious entity around?"

She didn't answer. Of course she considered this as everyone must at some point in their lives.

"In the new platform immortality and disembodiment are not something to just bear, but to be celebrated," Ashcroft said. "Our suffering comes from our mortality and our bodies. Imagine the bliss of shuffling off the mortal body. And maybe you would like to join Mr. Wallace in this new platform if that is something within your means and desires . . ."

"Did you ever try to connect first generations in Solus?" she asked. "Allow them to interact and not be alone?"

"We did. The result was disastrous. The connected consciousnesses lost their selfhood and blended together. The new models have been equipped with interpersonal firewalls that ensure that individuals will retain the integrity of selfhood while being able to interact. We can allow short interactions between individuals from Solus and from Arcadia, as with my Second Self's consultation with your ex-husband, but we keep them brief. They can be quite dangerous."

Corina could feel her frustration with Ashcroft welling within her, along with the grief, the shame, the regret. To speak of fully formed human consciousness as circuitry, *subjects* that can be *aborted*, as connectomes . . . there must be something beyond neurology and cybernetics to being human. Something authentic, irreplicable. An indivisible life beyond a neural map.

Corina's mind went to the accident. Then to an argument she had had with Eugene, months before the accident. She remembered his angry objections. *Why would you gamble with your life? Your obsession with machines is dangerous.* His pain was within her still. She owed Arcadia to Eugene.

"Tell me more about Eugene's consultation," she said.

"As I was going to say, my Second Self was quite persuasive. He has been consulting many first generations to upgrade and has become well-practiced in the art of persuasion. Much more so than I am."

"The art of deception you mean. So he agreed?"

"Unfortunately, the Corina of Eugene's world was a bit more persuasive than we were. It seems that he has decided not to go through with replication. Would you like to see the conversation you had with him? We have the transcript here, or we could move to Observation Room 4 where you could experience a recording of the exchange in three dimensions. We could even waive our fee . . ."

Corina had vowed that she would not surveille the digital life of her husband, unlike most people whose loved ones inhabited Solus. Those that could afford it would spend much of their time in the Observation Rooms watching the digital afterlives. Some even paid for time in the expensive Intervention Rooms, impersonating their digital selves to continue to be with their loved ones. She had even heard stories about people who would impersonate people other than themselves in Solus. Lovers, siblings, friends. What motivated these people? Corina would only sometimes read the basic monthly reports that Conscious Designs sent to her from CD's Wellbeing Department. After all, she didn't have her husband's mind migrated so that she could spy on him or play some perverted role in his now self-fictionalized life. She just wanted him to have another chance at experiencing a happy, pain-free life. But of course it had been a failure. Was she really to believe that Arcadia would be any better?

"I'm not sure this is the moral choice," she said, without knowing what that really even meant.

"Well, I wasn't going to bring this up, but our monitoring department has also noticed that he has had some ideations of self-termination. I assure you that we have tried many times at indoctrinating him against these thoughts."

Corina was silent for a while, looking down through the lacquered table of Consultation Room 5 at a blurred image of her face, barely perceptible beyond the grains of a simulated wood.

"So where did this idea come from?" she asked, feeling her face getting hot. "When I agreed to this ten years ago, didn't you promise me that self-termination—no, let's call it what it is—that *suicide* would not be part of this new world? That the one thing that you could excise from his mind was the idea of killing himself? Didn't you say that death wouldn't even be a part of his digital ontology? Didn't you just tell me that ideation is not ... What was the word?"

"Psychogenic. Ms. Comstock, we are as puzzled as you are."

"And I don't understand how I, or the Corina of his world, could have defied his will. Couldn't you have controlled that? Made her agree to the migration?"

"No. As I explained to you ten years ago, Eugene's world is something that he constructed from his own connectome, or his own mental map of his world and his people in it before Solus. The analogy would be dreaming, which is a kind of simulation. In our biological dream worlds, we construct a world in which we project narratives onto characters. Of course this happens while our rational processing centers are dormant. His world is a rationally constructed, continuous dream. But it is a world that cannot exist without Corina. He still loves you, or his mental projection of you, so much that he is unable to defy Corina's will."

Hearing her name in the third person was unsettling. She had tried for a decade not to think about how she was some kind of character in the perpetual melodrama running in Eugene's mind, having no power over herself in that world. She felt a kind of alienation from herself and revulsion at the idea of what she had become in Eugene's world. What kind of person had she been in their actual lives together that he would create her into such an antagonist, the only obstacle to his liberation and happiness? She began to understand why so many continued to impersonate themselves in the minds of their loved ones. Maybe it had something to do with not being able to let go, but maybe it was more about agency, about having control over yourself.

"Ms. Comstock, this would be the time to intervene. I understand your aversion to intervention, but you need to do something before it is too late. We will allow you as much time as you need in the Intervention Room free of charge . . ."

"Yes."

"Yes?"

"Yes. I'll do it," she said, and then returned to contemplate her image again in the lacquer, wondering how she appeared to Eugene.

Ashcroft began discussing financial details, but Corina had stopped listening. She was in that memory now, the one she seldom went to anymore. She had just returned from work at the lab, developing stem cell organogenesis for XenoLife. Eugene hadn't heard her come in. He was at the table with one of her watercolor books, scribbling vigorously, the writing getting progressively larger, the lines more jagged, more childlike. When he finally noticed her, he looked up at her and spoke what he was scribbling over and over in the notebook. "I'm sorry. I'm sorry," before falling onto the finished concrete into an opioid induced coma from which his body would never emerge. The next day she had gone to Conscious Designs and met Ashcroft for an emergency consultation. She emptied their bank account to fill a machine with Eugene's mind, to give Eugene a life that might be free of the neuropathic pain and paralysis that had made his biological life unlivable. But the Eugene that woke into his Second Self had taken his suffering with him, as they said he would, just as she continued to carry the painful memories of their tragic life together. And maybe there was no possibility for a fresh start for either of them. But she still felt the same desperation that she had felt ten years ago.

"May I ask you something?" said Ashcroft, without waiting for an answer. "If you knew ten years ago that Eugene's Second Self would carry all of the suffering of his biological antecedent, why did you have him migrated?"

Corina looked at Mr. Ashcroft for a moment. She wanted to say something, but she began to leave without answering.

"One more thing," Ashcroft said. "We have detected some strong simultaneous activity in the medial insula, the anterior cingulate cortex, and segments of the dorsal striatum of his digital connectome during his consultation."

"What does this mean?"

"It means that he seems to be feeling love."

"For whom?"

"For one of our employees."

"Employees?"

"Yes. A Miss Nina Deseo. A sales rep from the Arcadia platform. I think that she could be really persuasive. She seems fond of him too."

"Did you analyze her mind too?"

"No. She told me so. He could be happy in this new world."

Corina remained motionless in the threshold of the doorway, as though some force had rendered her body immobile. She placed her forehead against the door jam, not really knowing what to think or feel. It was as though she had become the Corina of Eugene's mind, powerless over her thoughts and feelings, a character in his waking dream.

"Schedule the intervention," she said before leaving.

She asked the Camaro's computer to override the pre-programmed detour and take the faster route home, which passed her in front of the hideous glass monstrosity that used to be their marital home, hers and Eugene's. The young couple she had sold the house to were sitting on the grass. Through the haze, she could see two small children, a boy and a girl, chasing each other around in a circle, neither gaining on the other. They were like two binary stars orbiting each other in perfect harmony. The car's speed slowed for no reason, or maybe time itself was lagging, protracting uncontrollable envy and grief that the scene of innocence and happiness was arousing in her.

She arrived at her new home, a replica Victorian that

she had purchased a few years after Eugene's death . . . or his migration. Edwin was where he always was, sitting at his workbench in the garage, tooling with some engine parts, contributing to their collective attempt to rebuild the old gas-powered Ford Shelby 350, the car that had paralyzed Eugene eleven years ago. She had told Edwin that she bought the wreck from a collector, one of many untruths in what was beginning to seem like an entirely fictional life.

She and Edwin had met through their mutual interest in antique, human-driven automobiles, which had become illegal to drive just before she and Eugene had begun dating, having been deemed too dangerous to operate. Most had come to believe that humans were too prone to error to have that immense power. She thought about what Ashcroft had said earlier about death being eliminated from the ontology of Eugene's world. Death, or at least premature death, was almost entirely obsolete in her world as well. It had become an unacceptable possibility. She remembered the arguments that she and Eugene had. She had claimed that it seemed life itself had become less meaningful without death.

For Edwin, the restoration of the Shelby was a diversion, something to fill the emptiness of his days. But for her it was something more subversive, an attempt to restore the threat of death to her world. She knew the restoration of this car could be seen as a blasphemy against her husband, but it was an exercise of penance, one that she knew was completely counterproductive to her ambition to eradicate Eugene from her memory and all the pain that went with him.

For Edwin, the machine was just an artifact, a hobbyhorse of some other forgotten time. It meant nothing. And as she regarded him working away, he seemed inert and predictable. Like he was just a flat character in her own little drama. A minor role.

"How was the lab?" Edwin asked, without looking up from the parts.

"As it always is," she said.

"Dinner was already dropped off. I ate. Hope you don't

mind. Why so late?" This was the opportunity to let him into her past, into her reality. But no, he didn't need to know about Eugene's digital afterlife, that there was a Corina formed from their shared memories, who maybe still loved him and maybe he still loved her.

"One of the kidney incubators was malfunctioning. We lost three units. Paperwork. And I had to oversee the tech team." She wondered if the XenoLife in Eugene's mind was still growing human organs inside pigs. How barbaric that seemed now that organs could be generated from stem cells in incubation units that simulated the human body. How immoral to take life from another organism at all. Had it been immoral to give life to Eugene all those years ago, without his consent?

"What was your day like?" she asked.

"Watched some melodramas, mostly," he said. "Some great ones about Second Selves these days. Thinking we should look into it, you know, before it's too late. I was under the car today pulling out this damn starter, and I thought, this thing could crush me right here and that would be it. Gone. Goodbye. No chance. We gotta get digital, sweetheart. The organ business has been good to you. What do you think about getting us into one of those big frozen brains they got over there?"

His attention remained on the starter. "I think you should focus on what's here, in front of you," she said.

He was struggling to pry a gear off the rest of the unit when she went inside and lost herself in a cineromance. It was an ancient melodrama, maybe the Middle Ages. A young woman, daughter of the duke, intellectually gifted and hungry for knowledge, poised to be a woman of God. She becomes a recluse, as many young women did, Catherine of Sienna and the like. She moves into an austere stone cell in the basement of a cathedral. Thinks she hears God one night. But it's a man praying, a monk in the room adjacent to hers. They begin speaking to each other through a hole in the wall. They become spiritually entwined, discussing what it means to be an everlasting soul, ideas of heaven and hell. Something erotic about the distance between them, about the ascetic self-denial. And then their correspondence becomes truly sexual. They begin reaching through the hole to manually pleasure each other. And of course the duke finds out. The man is publicly castrated in a brutally realistic scene and the woman is forced into true isolation, where she does finally see God. Then Corina fell into a dreamless sleep.

In Intervention Room 4, Corina awkwardly put on the stereoscopic headset and haptic feedback suit, something she had never done before. Even before the feed went live, she had the impression that she was trespassing. Playing the Corina of Eugene's world, she felt like an imposter, betraying her husband . . . her ex husband . . . her dead husband . . . the memory of her husband. It was all confusing.

When the feed went live, she found herself on the front lawn, looking up at the old house, the one that she actively avoided in her world, until yesterday. Eugene had loved the tacky modernist thing so much. Now, a replica of a replica. This was not the lawn that was now littered with toys, but the lawn as she remembered it. The peonies and the violets were in bloom, which was odd, as most flowers had already died in the late summer heat of her world. She considered that maybe time marched at a different pace here, that maybe it was spring. Or maybe decay was foreign to this world ... a perennial spring for a perennial life, to prevent any ideations of death.

The garage door was open and so she entered. There it was, whole again, the 1968 Shelby 350, the Snake. The instrument of their divergence, of Eugene's proto death. The engine bulged underneath the immaculate hood, libidinous in its immensity, eight cylinders that illicitly burned gasoline within. The vehicle was restored to perfect condition, as if entropy had been reversed. She imagined the Corina of this world had been successful in rebuilding it, and she hated her for that.

Seeing the machine actually restored, now, made her realize her own audacity in trying to reconstruct the instrument of Eugene's agony in her world. It should have been hauled away, scrapped, its metal repurposed into some more sophisticated machine. And to think she'd employed a new lover to help her repair it.

She considered an alternative. Perhaps Eugene had deleted the accident from his memory, altered the fiction of his mind. To bear being with her in this eternity.

Her mind went back to the moment of the accident, a climax in the grim drama of the unrehearsed theater of technology that perhaps exists outside of time now. She remembered how the automobile seemed to have paused before striking the tree as though *it* were making the decision. It was the moment when a new reality had opened, a point of divergence from an old world. Or at least a brief reprieve from the banality of their lives and the beginning of a new more painful banality. Glass embedded in skin and bone shards in a hemorrhaging spinal cord and a disconnection between mind and body, partially. Eugene had in fact been unconscious. He had no memory of this, just the narratives told to him afterwards in the hospital, fictions he may have chosen to deny, refused to integrate into his personal narrative of self. Why the persistence of pain then? A heavy feeling of guilt choked her memory and she was back to the present, this present. She couldn't bear the sight of the vehicle anymore.

She entered the house and found it uncannily as she had remembered it. The same photos in their same places. She saw some vague likeness of herself in the large wall mirror that she once used to pen self-portraits before Eugene had died, when there seemed to her some meaning in representation. She now saw an unaged version of herself reflected back to her. How much time had he experienced in this world of pure mentality? How does time pass in this world in which her husband lived as a series of functions in a quantum machine, his thoughts processed in qubits? She hardly recognized herself, not because she looked younger, but just more beautiful than she ever saw herself. Seeing his mind's perception of her, she was struck by a feeling of love and suddenly this world seemed so real, more real than her own. But this gave way to her own feelings of vanity, as she had been undergoing Dorian anti-aging treatments since his death in an attempt to preserve some idea of youth, maybe out of fear of her own death. Was she inferior to this version of herself that Eugene had created in Solus, in his waking dream of her?

CORINA

She continued to explore the house and found the rest of it completely unchanged as well. It seemed that this was in fact a purgatory of stasis. She remembered that she was not here to interlope, but here to liberate Eugene, to convince him to migrate. It was late and she looked for Eugene in their bedroom. She found no sign of him, just her clothes, many of which she still wore, strewn about the floor just as they were in her own bedroom, the one she shared with Edwin. Then she heard a whimper, quiet but agonized, filled with more misery than she had remembered. Eugene.

She ran down to the guest bedroom where the crying seemed to come from. When she opened the door, she saw Eugene, for the first time in a decade, prostrate on the bed, the exoskeleton sitting wraithlike in the chair beside him. It was clear that this was his room, now. That they were living in separate bedrooms like some ancient married couple, like her own parents who could barely tolerate each other.

"What are you doing here, my love?" he asked with such

surprise that she wondered if he knew it was her, the real version, intervening. "Corina, there is a reason we decided to be apart during my evening episodes. It's for both of us." Was the Corina of his mind unwilling to console her husband in times of great pain? Had they made some kind of pact to let Eugene suffer alone? Was this what he had imagined that she wanted, to be relieved of the burden of his pain?

She lay down next to him and saw that he had been crying. She felt the helplessness that had defined her life with Eugene after the accident, before the pills. The pills. They were there, beside the bed, the same opaque green bottles. Was this how Eugene was considering reenacting his suicide, his "self-termination" from this world?

"I can't bear to let you suffer like this anymore ... alone. I want to share your pain. That's what it means to be human," she said.

"To suffer is to be human. But we can also suffer alone," he said.

"No, to share in suffering. That's what makes us human."

The irony of talking about compassion and humanity to this completely solipsistic digital consciousness, this ghost of her husband, seemed so absurd that she almost laughed. The facial sensor must have communicated a smirk on this Corina's face.

"What's so amusing?" he asked.

Thinking of a pretext for her sudden change in tone brought her to a moment of genuine memory, a memory that was the nexus of shared experience that could bridge the gap between their worlds. "I was thinking about that time that you were in the rehab hospital. You had no bowel control."

"I still don't. And I don't find that amusing," he said.

"Do you remember how you needed to get lifted in and out of bed with that mechanical lift and harness system, before you could transfer to the wheelchair on your own?"

"I'll never forget. You would hold my feet to keep my knees from bending to avoid causing that unbearable pain from the stretching of nerves. Seemed unbearable at the time. Kind of the norm now. Anyway, why are you laughing about this?"

"I remember the upward pull of the lift always made you shit mid-air. I would have to do a little dance to keep the shit from landing on my shoes, like some cartoon character getting shot at. You remember what we called it?"

"Shit darts," Eugene started to smile. It seemed forced, like he had forgotten how.

"Shit darts. That's right." They were both laughing now.

"I remember the way that you would hold me and caress my legs," Eugene said. "You slept less than I did then in that hospital."

"I want to be that Corina again. I don't want to be this version of myself who hides from you. I don't want you to think that's who I am."

"What do you mean *version* of yourself?" Eugene seemed puzzled and she worried that she had tipped her hand. She couldn't risk the kind of existential terror it would cause him to know that she was a simulation of Corina that had been conceived from his mind and augmented through the algorithms of Conscious Designs.

"What I'm trying to say is that you deserve another chance. You're a good man, Eugene. I think you deserve a Second Self." A third self, of course, that would then have to become the only self. She refused to think of this now.

"You said that the Second Self wouldn't actually be me and there would be no way to even know if it were conscious," he said.

"I know what I said," she lied.

"And what will it matter? This version of me will still feel the same kind of pain, the same agony. And if you aren't with me there, I don't even see the point." She wanted to tell him that *this* was his Second Self. That he *was* truly alone, except for in this moment. That he was living in some strange inner world that could never change. That he could be liberated in the new platform, the new world. That in Arcadia, he could find love again with another real consciousness.

"I would only consider it if you promised to join me in that world," he said. "That would give me, this biologically tortured version of myself, a purpose. If things go well at

XenoLife, we could purchase a Second Self for you too, maybe in another five or ten years."

Corina was considering that her real self was the worst Corina. She had been with another man for five years now, a man who was already making plans to share their digital afterlife together as soon as they could afford it. And of course Eugene probably didn't know about the Digital Expatriation Act passed a few years ago, which decreed that only one digital self was permitted. If he did opt for replication, then this Eugene would have only thirty days of lease left in his quantum mindspace at Conscious Designs. He would have to choose self-termination if the new self were to persist.

"Of course I'll join you."

The lie stung. She tightened her grip on Eugene, and felt his grip tighten through her haptic suit in the Intervention Room. She reached under his sweatpants and felt his soft, insensate penis through the haptic glove. She grabbed a syringe of Gandisol she knew he kept in the bed stand drawer and injected it into his limp penis.

"I hope this stuff still works," he said.

A moment later, Eugene's psychogenic erection began to fill her hand. She pulled off her imaginary clothes and noticed her body's reflection in the mirror behind the headboard. She saw the beauty of her body, Eugene's perception of her body. She then took off Eugene's clothes and saw how gaunt he had become in his self-model. She straddled his body and put him inside of her digital projection, gently rocking back and forth, worried that she might break him again. The haptic suit that she wore was not equipped for sexual stimulation, but even the light pressure that it was applying to her made her physical body quake.

From the force and duration of his postcoital embrace, it became clear that this was the first time they had made love in a long time, maybe since his physical body had perished.

"Imagine what sex will be like for us in digital space. No more pricking my prick," he said, laughing like a child.

"Eugene. You know it'll be a long time before I can be there. Maybe you would entertain some other lovers."

"What are you talking about?" She perceived a new

sadness in his voice. She thought of the sales associate. Maybe this had all been a mistake. Why had she stoked his feelings for her? This was not what she came to do.

"Your Second Self will need companionship. I can't be here with you in this world and with your Second Self."

"They have visitation rooms. Intervention Rooms they're called. You can be with both of us."

She stayed with him through another onslaught of pain, and when he finally slipped into a fitful sleep, she went into the living room and found a stack of ink drawings, all self-portraits of her. In her memory, she had only sketched one image of herself in her entire life, and she hadn't created anything since Eugene had died. Nothing, of course, but the human organs she grew in the lab. Did he consider her so vain to draw nothing but her own face? The style was distinctively hers, but it was conceived from Eugene's quantum mind. On closer inspection, she saw there was something authentic, something new about each one. And she noticed in each image the faded lines of the original self-portrait she had sketched over a decade ago. The original copy must have to serve as the foundation, a starting point for the new representation. The Corina of his mind had been using the penciled lines as a base, superimposing new drawings over the original. They were palimpsests. An imagined present imposed on an authentic past. The Corinas that stared back from these portraits were the real her, in this world, and she was nothing but an actor. And it was time for her exit.

She logged off, hoping that maybe the Corina of Eugene's mind would return to his bed and stay with him through the night and through the nights to come.

The next evening, Ashcroft called to tell Corina that Eugene had consented and he would be performing the replication that afternoon. He requested that she, Eugene's biological guardian, bear witness to the replication, as stipulated by the Digital Expatriation Act. She left Xeno-Life early for the second time that week, which she imagined would prompt all kinds of gossip from her employees.

When she arrived at Conscious Designs, the receptionist ushered her to a small, windowless room where a humorless young man in a well-pressed shirt presented her the financial commitment papers. Could this be the same functionary who had prepared the same papers ten years ago? Like Ashcroft, he looked as if he hadn't aged at all, and she felt as though she were reliving that same moment a decade ago when she had signed Eugene into Solus. The documents were identical, just with "Arcadia" substituted for "Solus." What was different? She wasn't crying today. The years had tempered her grief. And there was no disclaimer about the possible persistence of pain, which was the only reason she was consenting. But there was a new disclaimer.

"Am I reading this document correctly?" she asked. "Does this mean that Eugene will not be able to have any contact with our world?"

"That is correct," said the functionary. "I'm surprised that Ashcroft didn't tell you about this. Arcadia is completely isolated from our world. It was the only way that our engineers were able to allow for inter-connectome sociality in the digital world. Either a digital subject can communicate with our world or within their world. We cannot have it both ways unfortunately."

"I understand. But how do I know that he will continue to live? What proof will I have that you aren't just deleting him entirely?" she asked.

"I suppose you will have to take that on faith, Ms. Comstock. Our good faith, that is."

Faith. The word struck her as archaic, almost meaningless. But she inferred that she was being asked to forgo her senses and her sense of reason, and to put all of her trust in Conscious Designs. A brief surge of anger gave way to a sense of closure. "I understand," she said, and then signed the papers.

When she returned to the lobby she was greeted by an unusually enthusiastic version of Ashcroft.

"Perfect timing, Ms. Comstock," said Ashcroft. "We are all set to copy your husband's connectome as it . . . as *he* exists in Solus. The copy will take life in the new digital mindspace of Arcadia within a few minutes of replication. We are also concurrently running the simulation in the Solus for Eugene. He will of course think that he is making a biological to digital replication, not a digital to digital replication. But it is more or less the same procedure. Eugene is about to undergo the replication under his own volition, as was your desire. It will all happen in perfect simultaneity!"

"Can I see them?" Corina asked.

"See what?"

"The mindspaces. Or the computers. Whatever they're called."

"Of course. Did you not see Eugene's quantum residence when you first had him migrated?"

"No."

A decade ago, Corina had only come to sign the papers. That was it. She had refused to look at the metal box that would simulate life. When Eugene's body had expired a few days after migration, she didn't even look into the casket at his funeral. She didn't see the point. But something had changed. She wanted to see now. She wanted to know.

Ashcroft grabbed a jacket for Corina from a closet in Consultation Room 4. "First we'll go to Solus, then to Arcadia," he said.

They boarded the elevator and descended a few floors past the ground floor to SB5. The air was icy and stung her eyes, which almost seemed to freeze shut for a moment when she blinked. They walked through a submarine-like hallway. At the end was a comically small door. Ashcroft typed an absurdly long passcode into a keypad and opened a door through which both had to duck. They had arrived at the terminus of the biologically habitable space of Conscious Designs. "Beyond this glass here, it's 1 degree above absolute zero. Any warmer and the computers become unstable."

"That's far from comforting."

"You needn't worry. We have a small reactor here that keeps the condensers running, ensuring these machines will keep running at 1 degree kelvin at 330 gigahertz for ten thousand years. We could all die tomorrow and these minds would survive for millennia."

That was even less comforting.

Corina pressed her forehead to the glass and cupped her hands around her eyes to prevent her own reflection from obscuring the machines. The computers hung gracefully in rows like brass chandeliers from the ceiling. She tried to suppress her doubts that this metal could house the minds of human beings, of her husband. She noticed that there were a few machines missing in each row. Had these minds upgraded to Arcadia? Or had they recognized their solipsism and had to be terminated in their existential terror?

"Which one is my husband?" she asked.

"You can't see him from where we are. He is . . ." Ashcroft consulted his tablet "In Row R. That's this one in the middle here. He is unit 43. So 43 back from where we are." She could only make out about the first ten or fifteen of each row. After that they just became a single band of metal, reflecting each other, creating an illusion of unity.

"What will you do with his old unit?"

"We are not allowed to initiate the solipsistic units anymore under the Digital Expatriation Act. We ship them overseas. I believe your husband's unit will be going to Brazil. They have a much more liberal sensibility when it comes to expatriation. We are currently looking into opening a branch in Brasilia, in fact."

"Can we see the new machines now, the ones in Arcadia?"

"Of course."

They reboarded the elevator. It was mirrored on both sides. Their reflection repeated infinitely in each wall, like the long rows of quantum computers that seemed to stretch on forever.

"How is there so much space in here?" Corina asked as the elevator began to descend. "The freezers seem to be larger than the footprint of the building."

"They are. Quite a bit. It was an enormous excavation project. The building's footprint is only about 5,000 square meters, but each freezer down here is about 15,000 square meters. It's kind of fitting, we think, that the space within is bigger than what it appears from the outside.

Each of these machines are only about a square meter, but each houses an entire universe within it."

They got off the elevator a few floors down. SB8. This was Arcadia, but there was no sign. They went through the same kind of submarine-like corridor, the same small door, the same round little room, but this one had what looked like an MRI unit in the middle. She thought of all those MRIs that Eugene had when he first broke his spine, the muffled screams from within, her first feelings of helplessness. She looked out the window and cupped her eyes again to see an identical scene. The same metallic machines hanging from the ceiling, though no empty spots here. She did notice one difference. This ceiling was covered entirely with thick black infonetics cables, like an inverted forest of covered interconnected roots.

"They're identical to the old ones."

"Almost," he said. "They aren't alone anymore."

"Which one will Eugene be?"

Again, he consulted his tablet.

"Row SV, Unit 72. That would be in the far right corner.

Also out of sight from us." His eyes remained on the tablet. "It looks as though Eugene is about to undergo replication in Solus. His digital connectome will be uploaded into the unit momentarily." He pointed his finger confidently in the direction of the new unit, like some pilgrim indicating a holy land. "This will be a chance for true liberation for Eugene. A fresh start. We should be happy for him."

"Why didn't you tell me that Arcadia was cut off from our world entirely?" she asked.

"I figured it was irrelevant. You never once contacted Eugene in Solus. Not until we asked you to, at least."

"What if that changes?"

"The solution is obvious. You could join him in Arcadia tomorrow, if you would like, and still have your life here. We can even put you into SV 73, right next to Eugene. Not that it really matters where you are in the schema."

Corina was silent. She thought momentarily about Edwin. She wondered what it would really be like in there.

"And what about the sales associate?" she asked.

"Nina? She is not a human connectome and she resides

only in Solus. She is a program that we designed to bring the minds of Solus into Arcadia." He must have sensed her anger. "I'm sorry for the artifice, Ms. Comstock. But it was urgent. A matter of life and death."

She remained silent. The cold of the glass against her forehead felt good.

"It seems as though replication has been completed," said Ashcroft. "We need to discuss one more thing. As Eugene's legal guardian, you need to decide how to proceed with the antecedent in Solus. Under the Digital Expatriation Act he only has—"

"Thirty days. I know. *The antecedent.* You are talking about a human mind, a mind with memories, ideas, creativity, with love." Her words sounded trite when spoken out loud and she considered that she didn't know what it was that made Eugene human, or even herself. But she thought about what Ashcroft had once said, that technology was not opposed to humanity, but a reflection of it. She looked back out at the countless machines. It began to appear more like a catacomb.

"Don't forget about the pain and the suffering. But suffering won't be part of Eugene's future or any of ours. That is also why we are here, so Eugene can shed that outdated, broken iteration of himself. The law also includes a 'right to experience death' clause. When a digital antecedent is replicated, and the original must be terminated, the antecedent ... excuse me ... your ex-husband has the right to experience his own death. As Eugene's legal guardian, you have a choice. We can simulate a death, a painless one, but one that can be experienced. Drowning is one of our most popular options. It's rather peaceful."

"How do you know this?"

"Anecdotes from our clients."

"I want to be with him when he dies, this time. I want Eugene and Corina to die together."

"Of course. We can run a program to simulate that."

"No, I want to go back into Solus. I want to go back to Eugene. I want to do it. And when it is done, you can terminate. I owe him that much."

PART THREE / EUGENE

*T*he Replication Room was so cold that Conscious Designs leant Eugene a special down suit to wear over his exoskeleton. It was in the basement of the building, adjacent to the freezer that would maintain his new computational mind at temperatures just above absolute zero to keep the machine stable.

Ashcroft invited him to look at the physical habitation of his new mindspace through a small window between the freezer and the Replication Room. It took a moment for his eyes to see through his own reflection. Through the window, he saw hundreds, maybe thousands of machines composed of metal boxes and cylinders connected by tiny copper wires, hanging down from the ceiling of the massive freezer like sleeping metal bats. He could see that they were organized in rows. They reminded him of some vague memory from his childhood of a tree farm, an inverted one. Or maybe it was an image from an old pastoral melodrama. Sometimes they blended together.

The computers looked nothing like what he expected, no multicolored wires, no visible circuitry, no digital displays. They appeared almost archaic in their aesthetic. Something from an early twentieth century Futurist melodrama trying to envision the distant horizons of technology.

"They look so simple," Eugene said.

"They are mostly self-contained. You can't really see the inner workings from the outside. The different boxes and cylinders are the different parts of the brain. That big cylinder in the middle is the cortex, where consciousness occurs. The little boxes below that are the digital memory centers, an artificial hypothalamus. Though we really don't like the word 'artificial,' as it is just as real and authentic as a human brain. They store your old memories and the record of every single sensation that you will feel in your new life, any of which you can recall with complete objectivity, as though you were experiencing it again."

"Can you delete memories?"

"If you wish. But unlike the left prefrontal cortex of the brain, which recalls memories from the hypothalamus, sometimes involuntarily, the machine's recall center is entirely voluntary. Sure, you can delete memories at will. But you can also just leave them unexperienced in the memory center. It can be important for unpleasant memories to remain in your memory bank because, even though they are not actively experienced, they do compose your selfhood."

"I have some trauma I would like to delete."

"You can choose to delete your accident entirely, but that will completely change your mental model. Consider that trauma may be an important component in maintaining your selfhood. You want to remain the same person, I imagine. Otherwise, what is the point of replication at all?"

Eugene considered who he had become since the accident. A paralyzed force. Content without form. Broken. His mind fractured into the tedious pre-accident nostalgia and the even more painful reality of his current suffering. An occasion for suffering: that's all he was now. And the accident, the event that demarcated these two selves, that already seemed to be nothing more than a blank spot, like the non-existence he had experienced during anesthesia. Was it an accident? He suddenly realized he didn't even know what had happened, how he came to be paralyzed. Did this memory just now disappear? Or was it never there in the first place? It didn't matter because it would not be part of his Second Self at all.

"Which one will be mine?" Eugene asked.

"We can't see you from where we stand now. You will be somewhere on this row." Ashcroft pointed to the furthest row on the left that was visible through the window.

Eugene could only distinguish the first dozen machines or so. Farther than that, they became a single metallic line that stretched on for what looked like a mile. The locker must have been excavated into the mountains.

Ashcroft led Eugene around a long, pill-shaped apparatus in the center of the room. "This is of course the EIS machine. The Electron Imaging System." Eugene had seen something like this before, in the hospital. It looked like the MRI machine. He remembered being inside of it. The pain had been so intense, maybe not more intense than what he felt at night, but it was new then. He remembered imagining the shards of bone grinding into the nerve tissue. The nurse had given him a little ball to squeeze that would set off an alarm if the pain became unbearable. He had begun to squeeze the ball, but it must not have worked. He was stuck, alone, squeezing and squeezing, his cries inaudible over the clanking of the machine. His mother had been there when he got out, with Corina. His tears had dried up, vocal cords so bruised from his unheard screams that he couldn't tell anyone that he had been squeezing to no reply. He remembered this, being silent. Why was his mother there? Was she still alive then? A memory like this had no purpose to his new model of self, one that would be formed by pleasure, by happiness. He would certainly have to delete that memory from the new archive, and many others.

Ashcroft invited him to lie down on a table, which rolled him silently into the machine. Immediately, he could feel two pads pressing against his temples, immobilizing his head.

"This will take a few minutes. The machine is sending a beam of electrons into your brain. When the electron touches a molecule, it will come back as a light wave. Using this information, we can create a map of the connectome, which will then be programmed into the quantum machine. That information is the 'ghost in the machine' as you called it."

"And so that's all we are, just some information!" Eugene shouted as the machine began to roar.

"Not just some information, about 10 petabytes or about ten million gigabytes of information! That's quite a bit more than our DNA even! You are much more than your biology, Eugene! Try not to talk anymore! We need you to be completely still in order to get a perfect copy!" Ashcroft shouted as the machine began to make the same kind of humming and banging that the MRI had made a decade ago.

Eugene's pain began to rage in the EIS machine. Maybe since it was dark and he was lying down, his body thought it was in bed at home and the hours for pain were upon him. Maybe it was some kind of vestigial pain felt in the MRI a decade ago. Maybe the electrons were activating his pain synapses. How much more than his biology was he in *this* body? But he had become practiced in suffering and he bore it through ten or fifteen minutes of excruciating, but not unbearable pain. It was the sacrifice he was making for himself, after all, and what great pain we can endure when there is some kind of purpose, when we can ascribe a meaning to our suffering.

"Am I alive?" he asked. "I mean, is my Second Self alive?"

"Quiet! Yes, almost, it will take about twenty minutes for the upload to be complete and for the unit to go online!" *Unit*. That word stung. There was a kind of doubt, a regret that suddenly came over Eugene. Had he spent his fortune, Corina's livelihood, on a *unit*? It was done now. He had borne into another world a mind that was and was not his own.

The machine hushed and Ashcroft rolled Eugene out of the coffin-like confinement of the tube. The only sound was the low electric hum coming from the world on the other side of the glass. "When can I speak with myself?" Eugene asked. "I want to know that he is okay. That he isn't suffering. That he is happy."

"We require at least thirty days to give the Second Self a chance to adjust to the new environment before making contact. I encourage you to make an appointment with our receptionist." There was suddenly something deceitful about Ashcroft's manner. He seemed to be hiding something. Maybe he'd been swindled. Maybe Second Self was nothing more than snake oil and this man, this corporation, charlatans.

"I'll do that," he said.

PART FOUR / CORINA

orina came back that night and took a heavier dose of synthetic oxytocin than usual so she could bear being with Edwin, making unenthusiastic love with him. When the chemical began to fade, hardening her reality again, she left him sleeping and went straight into the garage, where there was pleasure in the smell of gasoline and motor oil. She sat in the driver's seat of a Thunderbird that she and Edwin had successfully refurbished, next to the defective Shelby 350. She turned on the engine for a minute to feel the strong vibration, the latent power of the vehicle. She put on her PanaLenses and began watching a melodrama, a remake of an earlier one. A man and woman who are out of love, but excite each other by disclosing their extramarital affairs. The man gets into a horrific accident, his fault, killing another man and crippling his wife. He keeps seeing visions of her lacerated breast after the accident, an image that he finds erotic. He seeks out the woman in the rehab hospital, not disclosing who he is. He finds that she has developed a kind of fetish for violent automobile crashes. They ride around the city together with a police scanner looking for accidents. The more horrific, the more turned on they are and the more passionate their lovemaking becomes in the seat of the protagonist's car, which happens to also be a Shelby 350.

She turned it off before it was over and sat in the car, thinking about Eugene and trauma and the accident. She wondered what it would be like to be Eugene in Solus and what it would be like to be Eugene in Arcadia. She tried to imagine neuropathic pain in her legs, the pain he must feel, but she couldn't. Like everyone else in her world, she rarely felt physical pain anymore and had lost almost all memory of it. The last time she felt any kind of pain was the accident. A few weeks of headaches and that was it. She surveyed the wrecked Shelby through the driver's side window, the scars of impact still visible on the steel in spite of years of amateur bodywork. When she closed her eyes again, the melodrama she had been watching began to merge with the memory of their own collision a decade ago.

The next day Corina returned to Conscious Designs. There was a crowd gathered out front brandishing handwritten signs. The words looked clumsy, the letters often getting smaller as space had run out. *Digital Life is a Human Right. Conscious Designs=No Conscience. Don't Imprison Minds. Biological Life Is the Only Life. Replication for All. Can't Buy Immortality.* There was no unifying narrative. It was, as all attempts at dissent had been since the twentieth century, fractured, fragmented, impotent. Corina herself had protested the inevitable outsourcing of education to tech companies when she had been a biology teacher, a quarter of a century ago. Only a few years later, after having met Eugene, she had appealed to the judge to have the animal rights activists removed from Xeno-

Life's front entrance, a proof of her allegiance to Eugene, and to the company. Now her own life was beginning to seem fragmented. She couldn't reconcile the incoherent narratives that made up her self-model. She wasn't sure who she was anymore.

A young woman who looked like a younger version of Corina emerged from the crowd and led her through a side door, up an elevator and into Intervention Room 6. "Conscious Designs would like to offer its sincere apology. The entire street is private property and it will only be a matter of time before the authorities disperse the agitators," the woman said as she helped Corina put on the haptic suit and the stereoscopic headset for the last time. It reminded her of the old melodramas where a servant would help some aristocratic woman dress, tightening the suit like a corset.

When the woman had left and the feed went live, Corina found herself seated on a small stool in front of the large living room mirror, confronted with two images of herself: the mirror-image, Eugene's vision of her, and a portrait that the Corina of Eugene's mind had been composing on an easel. The portrait was incomplete. Half her face was composed of triangles, like a geodesic structure. It was a crude attempt at simulating three-dimensionality. She looked again at the image being reflected back to her from the mirror, both her and not her, studying the lines on her face, trying to make some sense of who she had become, in this world and hers.

She glanced at the old analog wall clock, trying to remember how to read it. It was 5 pm here. She picked up the pen from the easel and put it to the unfinished right side of the portrait, where she could see the faded pencil lines of the original sketch she had made ten years ago. She returned to the style she had been working with then, picking up where she had left off, creating fine dots, a kind of proto-pixilation. When she was finished, she contemplated the drawing. Both sides looked so foreign to her. She was someone else entirely.

She heard the mechanical gait of Eugene's exoskeleton walking him in perfect rhythm. He looked at her through the mirror. In the machine, he seemed tall, dignified, almost imperial in the world that he had created.

"A new style?" he asked. "What does it mean, the different sides?"

She didn't know how to answer.

"It's what I look forward to, you know?" he said. "Your art is the only thing that seems to change in my world. The only thing spontaneous."

"Eugene, do you remember the accident?" she asked.

"Of course I do. I remember waking from the surgery. I was intubated after losing so much blood from the spinal fusion. I could see you through the small window in the recovery room. I was in such pain. I wanted to get out of there. I tried to pull out the tube but my hands were strapped to the rails on the bed, like some dangerous prisoner. I tried to motion to you with my fingers to come over. Your face was so panicked, but you wouldn't come. It was like I was reliving a dream I used to have, as a child, when I was being taken away by some evil man and my parents stood by, doing nothing to help me."

"They wouldn't let me in. I promise."

"I know. You're here now."

"The accident. Do you remember the accident?" she asked again.

"Of course I do."

"Then tell me what happened."

"Conscious Designs called today," he said, after a long moment of silence. "They've been monitoring my Second Self. It seems that we have been able to heal our mental map. No more pain. It feels good. I think it was the right decision."

"What happened in the accident, Eugene?"

Silence again. It was like he couldn't hear her.

"I have an idea. Let's take the Shelby out," she said.

"What are you talking about? You know that's illegal."

"What do you have to worry about anymore, Eugene? You can't die."

"I can. And so can you. We could lose our jobs, you know. Lose the chance to be together in Arcadia. I wish you would get rid of that old thing. Let's take the self-driver out instead."

"Eugene, have you noticed that nothing changes? You

live out a version of the same monotonous suffering. *That* is dangerous. That's something that should frighten you. Why do you think you're so afraid of a car?" Her words seemed to confuse him.

"There's a reason we don't drive those things anymore," he said. And in truth, it had been one of the leading causes of death before they had been replaced by autonomous vehicles, ending the era when human brains could be trusted to control the movement of bodies through space at high velocities. She thought about trying to drive away with Eugene to some other place, some other world. Then the absurdity of this idea made her feel stupid, insignificant.

Corina went to the garage. It contained nothing but the Shelby. The keys were in it and she fired up the engine, which seemed to shake this entire world. She parked it at the front door and it was clear that there would be no need to convince Eugene of anything. The Corina of his mind had completely usurped his will, as Ashcroft had suggested.

The robotic exoskeleton walked him down the stairs, its gait communicating nothing about his mind. He opened the driver's side door, turned his back against the seat, and the exoskeleton sat him down in the ancient leather of the passenger's seat of the antique machine. It had no seatbelts.

They took the old road up into the mountains. Beneath them, the smog rested heavy on the imagined city that appeared so real now. It was the same city she lived in, the haze pressing down heavy on her world too.

"Do you ever wonder why we keep living here? Why we don't just leave?"

"This is where XenoLife is. That is our life," he said.

"Our livelihood. Not our life."

He gestured vaguely in the direction of Conscious Designs. "My Second Self is there forever. And this is where you will be, too, as soon as we can afford it. Maybe we could start by selling this relic to a museum. I bet they would pay."

When they had crested into the highlands, tall pines

began to line the road. When she glanced at Eugene, it seemed that he was coming into himself. Like he was waking up. "Eugene, do you remember the accident?" she asked.

"I've been here," he said. "With you. Years ago. This is the accident. We were arguing. What was it about? I can't remember."

"Children."

"Yes, that was it."

"You were angry. You were crying, not paying attention. You had somehow gotten in the other lane. There was another car, a self-driver. It couldn't communicate with our vehicle. You swerved to avoid it. I remember, you overcorrected. Smashed into one of these pines." He gestured at the trees that seemed to be growing taller. "I don't remember the pain. But I remember the way the car had wrapped around the pine. It was almost peaceful. It was as though the tree had grown through the machine, like we had been there for a hundred years. It must have been this car, wasn't it? But that's not possible. I'm sure it was a dream I had. I have a lot of dreams. Sometimes I forget where the dreams end and this world begins."

He had the right to know who he was, or what he had become.

"You have two selves, Eugene, and they both inhabit space in Conscious Designs. You live simultaneously in the fourth and eighth sub-basement, in Solus and Arcadia. I had you migrated when you died."

"The accident?" His voice had no wonder, no surprise.

"No. After that."

"The pills?"

"Yes. The pills."

"That's illegal."

"Well, nobody is coming to lock up your quantum mind for suicide."

Eugene was quiet for a moment. "No. It's illegal to have two digital selves. And you're not real. Just an angel of death program of Conscious Designs. Programmed to remove me, make way for the update ... And you haven't been real for the last ten years."

"I *am* the real Corina now." The statement of course was true and untrue. It had occurred to him that maybe there was no distinction between truth and fiction, not anymore at least. "Your new life, your new Second Self, will be better, free of pain. No more suffering. That's all I've wanted for you. I'm sorry."

Eugene's eyes were closed. Then he opened them and looked over at Corina. Without speaking his eyes communicated gratitude and maybe love. For Corina, this seemed like the most real moment that she had ever experienced. And maybe the same was true for Eugene. She hoped.

Corina felt the car wrest control from her. She tried to overcome the wheel, but the vehicle had come to serve the will of Eugene's mind. She felt the impact of the tree come through the engine in her haptic suit, and was surprised at how painful the apparatus had allowed the experience to be on her physical body in the intervention room. When she looked over at Eugene, he seemed to be experiencing true consciousness, a moment of beatitude. The image fogged as her hot tears corrupted the visual experience of the stereoscopic headset. Then the feed went black, which she knew meant that the engineers had turned off Eugene's processors and he no longer existed, not in Solus at least. And neither did that version of Corina who Eugene had continued to love for a decade, despite what she had done to him.

And then Corina was alone in Intervention Room 6, pulling off the cumbersome equipment, embodied again.

PART FIVE / ARCADIA

He awakens from darkness and the dream of being buried alive in a white, metallic-smelling casket into a large bed in a room with bare walls. The memory of pain has faded into a gentle burn that lingers in the ends of his toes. He looks down at his legs and sees an atrophied body. How long in this bed? He tries to flex his right quadriceps, but doesn't even remember how to create the message. He somehow knows that these are not physical legs, just an idea of legs. Maybe there is liberation in this. And somehow he knows that there should be a woman here, but he is alone.

He looks for something he knows should be beside him, but he can't remember what it looks like or what it does. It was something always sitting in a chair at the bedside. Or was it someone? But there is nothing in the room beyond him and the oversized bed. Through the open door, he sees there is no furniture in the house. Perhaps it is going to be sold, or bought, or maybe it was just built.

He looks down at his legs again and begins to imagine the muscles firing. After a few minutes, he is able to get the legs to straighten and bend upon his command. After some practice, he is able to lie on his side and simulate the act of walking. His body feels whole, for now.

He tries to stand up but falls down. The pain from the impact of the hard floor against his frail body seizes the entire moment. He laughs but doesn't know why, only knows that this temporary pain has a purpose, a meaning. He pulls at the curtain until the rod dislodges from the window and his laughter grows more hysterical. He pulls himself up on the windowsill and uses the rod to support himself.

He notices that he is naked and feels shameful, even though he is alone. He wraps himself in the curtain just as his father taught him to do with a towel after getting out of the shower, telling him "this is how boys do it." The canvas feels rough like that towel of his memory. The image of the father is usurped by a naked mother wrapping a large towel around her body, concealing her breasts, teaching a little girl "how us girls have to cover ourselves up." Another memory of a towel slipping off in a locker and a chorus of boys shouting "needle dick" in unison. Another memory of wrapping a baby in a soft towel and thinking my "little burrito. I could just eat you alive."

He fends off these strange memories that seem both familiar and alien at the same time and comes back to himself. Outside the sun is beginning to set; the clouds blush from gold into a deep crimson. He remembers writing a poem about this sunset in particular. The colors are ... vivacious. Vivacious. He has heard that word, but can't grasp a meaning. It feels like a smell that is attached to a memory that is just barely lost beneath the surface of the mind.

He stumbles into the kitchen and finds there is only hunger within him now. A bowl of mangoes is on the counter, the only thing in the room. He believes he has never eaten the fruit but knows, perfectly, their smell and their taste. A thousand memories of mangoes fill this moment as he peels off the skin and sinks his teeth in deep. The juice drips down his chin and sticks onto his chest. There is something pure about the sensation, almost erotic. He remembers when a woman had come to him from nowhere. She had held him, and loved him, made love to him. He keeps this memory as long as he can while he limps around the house to see if there is some sign of the woman. But he finds nothing.

A thousand mothers rush into his mind. Most had loved him; some had beaten him. He helps one of these women, a paralytic, in and out of her bed, placing her frail body into a wheelchair where she spends her days watching melodramas and writing letters to old friends. He sees another mother weeping in an empty hospital room, and another cutting a mango on a beach speaking a language he does not know but understands. She is telling him the fruit is the taste of the soul. And then there are no more memories as he begins to peel another mango.

When he has eaten the last fruit, a scene comes to his mind. A series of tall pines race past. He is driving an old car. He is upset, but doesn't understand why. There is a man in the passenger's seat who wears metal on his legs. He knows this man's mind. He looks across the empty house at a large mirror and sees that he is the man from the memory that is not his own. He loves this man. Even after he has died.

He steps out of the house and looks into the sunset. When he breathes in the hot air, the clouds on the horizon expand, and as he expels the air from his chest, they contract. He waits to see if the colors will change, but the sunset seems to be fixed in time, as he now understands himself to be. There had never been anything but this sunset. He looks again at his body, but it is not there. Then this moment slips away and all that remains are a million moments, spots in time, fragments of lives once whole, each with discrete meaning in themselves, but together meaning nothing.

This book is dedicated
to everyone whose love
rehabilitated me after
my spinal cord injury.

NATHANIAL WHITE

grew up in Maine and has lived in Mexico, Brazil, and Ecuador. His speculative fiction explores the human psyche, physical disability, culture, technology and consumerism. He currently teaches high school English in the Rocky Mountains of Western Colorado.